THE LIBRARY OF
EMERGENCY PREPAREDNESS™

FIRES AND WILDFIRES

A PRACTICAL SURVIVAL GUIDE

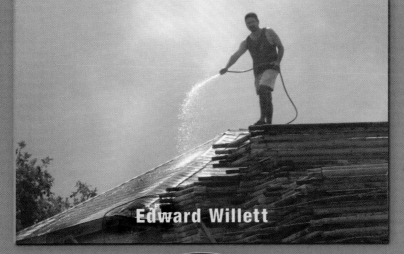

Edward Willett

rosen
central™

The Rosen Publishing Group, Inc., New York

Published in 2006 by The Rosen Publishing Group, Inc.
29 East 21st Street, New York, NY 10010

First Edition

Library of Congress Cataloging-in-Publication Data

Willett, Edward, 1959–
Fires and wildfires: a practical survival guide / Edward Willett.
     p. cm.—(The library of emergency preparedness)
Includes bibliographical references and index.
ISBN 1-4042-0532-2 (library binding)
1. Fires—Juvenile literature. 2. Wildfires—Juvenile literature. 3. Fire protection engineering—Juvenile literature. 4. Fire extinction—Juvenile literature.
I. Title. II. Series.
TH9148.W45 2006
363.37—dc22
                                                        2005015789

Manufactured in Malaysia.

On the cover: In October 2003, a homeowner hosed down the roof of his house to help protect it from a wildfire burning near Santa Paula, California.

CONTENTS

Introduction   4

1 Fire on the Loose   7

2 Home Fire Prevention
   and Preparedness   15

3 Wildfire Prevention
   and Preparedness   30

4 Escaping a Fire   36

5 After a Fire   49

   Glossary   55

   For More Information   57

   For Further Reading   59

   Bibliography   60

   Index   62

Introduction

In a fireplace on a wintry evening or at a campsite beneath the stars, fire is our friend. But when fire rages out of control, it's hard to imagine a more unyielding enemy.

In October 2003, the residents of Southern California discovered just how deadly fire can be. In a little more than a week, ten major fires consumed 800,000 acres (323,887 hectares), destroying more than 3,334 homes and claiming twenty-two lives. The total cost of the damage caused by the fires was estimated at $2 billion, making the fires the most expensive to ever hit the state.

More than 100,000 residents were forced to flee their homes. Among them was Vicki Clapp, a resident of Temecula. She described the experience in this excerpt from an interview with Karen Grigsby Bates for the National Public Radio program *Day to Day* on October 28, 2003.

I'd been speaking with my mother up in Big Bear a few minutes before this started, [Ms. Clapp said]. And my twenty-eight-year-old came in, grabbed me and said, "Mom, get things in the car. We've got to go." And I hadn't walked out and looked at how close it was. I grabbed medications first, I grabbed family photos, I grabbed my insurance policy for the house, I grabbed my address book and promptly set

Flames consume the living room of a home in San Diego, California, on October 26, 2003. Wildfires burned for days across parts of Southern California leaving twenty-two people dead and causing more than $2 billion in property damage.

it down on the table and forgot it. I turned around, I had a minute to look and see if there was anything else that was, you know, in my heart that I had to have. My set of tiny little inch-and-a-half wood ducks that were made for my grandparents I have been lucky enough to have; all the children have teethed on them and there's tremendous sentimental value. I grabbed those, stuck them in my pocket.

And when we evacuated our horses, the last trip was [so] stressful ... you couldn't see [the] two cars in front of us evacuating. My husband was behind me, my fifteen-year-old was in the bed of a truck behind him holding one of our goats, and you could hardly see. The smoke and the wind was blowing at least 50, 60 miles an hour [80 to 96 kilometers per hour]. And my husband stopped to pick up another horse that was tied to a fence and get it out. We only had two horses in our trailer, the last load we made, and he had room for this one. And it just—the sense of panic, to realize that he may be gone, and was abso—I was fine until that point, and I just absolutely fell apart.

[The family made it safely to a friend's house, where they spent the night.] And the first thing I pulled out of my pocket were these silly little ducks, and I said, "You know I've got everybody out, we've got the horses out and I've got my ducks, so I'm set."

As it happened, the family's home escaped the fire. But Ms. Clapp knew they were lucky. "…It was only because of the luck of the draw, the wind changing," she said. "When we left our home, I had no doubt we would have nothing left when we came back. And shortly afterwards, if the wind would have continued what it was doing, I would say we would have had fifteen minutes, maybe, and we would have been gone."

What would you do if your home was threatened by fire and you only had fifteen minutes to leave?

Statistically, you're likely to be affected by fire three times over the course of your life, either through personal experience or through the experiences of friends and family.

Will you be prepared?

1 --- **Fire on the Loose**

According to the National Fire Protection Association (NFPA), an international nonprofit fire prevention organization, there were 402,000 home fires in the United States in 2003. Those fires caused 3,165 deaths. Another 14,075 people were injured.

In 2000, one of the worst years for fires on record, wildfires across the western United States burned more than 5 million acres (2.02 million ha), destroyed 577 structures, and killed 8 people. Sadly, many of these fires were preventable—and some of the deaths and injuries that accompanied them could have been prevented if the victims had been better prepared.

How Home Fires Start

To know how to prevent fires, you need to know how they start. In order from most to least common, here are the top six causes of home fires:

- **Cooking fires:** Each year, on average, one out of every eight homes will experience a cooking fire. One common source is grease in an unattended frying pan.

- **Portable and space-heating equipment:** Whether they run on electricity or burn kerosene, wood, or propane, portable heaters can ignite flammable items that come in contact with them. These fires are particularly dangerous because they often start at night while members of the household are asleep.

- **Careless smoking:** Although cooking fires are the leading cause of home fires, cigarettes are the leading cause of fire deaths. That's because most smoking-related fires are caused by people smoking in bed. Smoldering cigarette butts that roll out of ashtrays or are tossed into trash containers can also start fires.

- **Faulty electrical wiring:** Because they lurk out of sight inside walls and ceilings, faulty electrical wires can cause fire with few, if any, warning signals. Faulty or cracked electrical cords and overloaded electrical outlets are other electrical fire sources.

- **Children with matches:** Playing with matches or lighters is the leading cause of fire deaths for children five years old and younger. Young children simply don't realize that fire is dangerous. However, they do know they're not supposed to play with matches. If they decide to play with them anyway, they often hide before doing so. That means the fires often start in closets or under beds, where there are lots of things that can burn—and where the children can get trapped.

- **Holiday hazards:** The winter holidays are a time when flammable trees and equally flammable decorations combine with seldom-used electrical cords and a proliferation of candles. Sometimes this causes disaster—especially when candles are left burning

Firefighters battled a blaze that destroyed a home in Scotts Bluff, Nebraska, in June 2005. Fire officials believe that faulty electrical wiring in the attic caused the fire.

unattended near combustibles. Illegal (and even legal) fireworks—including sparklers—also cause fires.

Conditions in a Fire

What are conditions like inside a burning building? You may imagine you know, but what you think you know is probably wrong, and if you don't have accurate information, you could be in danger. Here are the facts:

- **Fire is fast!** It takes less than thirty seconds for a small flame to get out of control and become a major fire. A house can fill with thick smoke in minutes and be engulfed in flame in just a few minutes more. Most fires occur when people are asleep. If you wake up and the house is on fire, you won't have time to grab valuables. There will only be time to escape—if you're lucky.

- **Fire is hot!** Flames are not the only thing that can kill in a fire. When a room is on fire, the temperature can be 100 degrees Fahrenheit (38 degrees Celsius) at floor level—and 600°F (316°C) at eye level. That kind of heat can scorch your lungs and melt your clothes. In just five minutes, a burning room can reach the flashover point, the temperature at which everything flammable ignites at once.

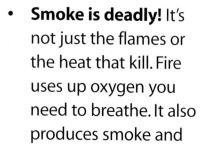
A firefighter gasps for air as he climbs through a second-floor window while smoke billows out behind him.

- **Fire is dark!** That doesn't sound right—after all, we light candles to illuminate dark rooms. But although a fire's flames are bright, the smoke it produces in a burning building is thick and black. Expect absolute darkness in a fire.

- **Smoke is deadly!** It's not just the flames or the heat that kill. Fire uses up oxygen you need to breathe. It also produces smoke and

🔥 A Fire-Safety Quiz 🔥

How much do you know about fire safety? Take this short quiz and find out (answers are at the end of the quiz, on page 12):

The number-one cause of home fires is:

 a. Cooking

 b. Smoking

 c. Candles

The most important way to protect your family from fire is:

 a. Live close to a fire station

 b. Don't have a fireplace

 c. Have working smoke alarms

Your house is on fire and you've made it outside, but your cat is still inside. You should:

 a. Go back for the cat.

 b. Hope the cat gets out on its own.

 c. Tell a firefighter where the cat might be.

You're frying hamburgers. When you step out of the kitchen for a minute, the grease catches fire. You should:

 a. Spray the fire with water.

 b. Carefully slide a lid over the pan to smother the fire and turn off the burner.

 c. Carry the frying pan to the back door and dump it outside.

(continued on following page)

A Fire-Safety Quiz

(continued from previous page)

Answers:

a. Cooking fires are the most common kind of home fires.

c. The National Fire Protection Association says that four-fifths of home fire deaths occur in homes without working smoke alarms.

c. Never go back into a burning building for any reason. That's the firefighters' job, if they judge it safe to do so.

b. Spraying water on a grease fire can spread it. Carrying it to the door may leave a trail of fire through the house.

toxic gases that can make you drowsy and disoriented, and can affect your breathing. Many people who have died in fires died in their beds because they were poisoned by gases before the fire ever reached their door.

- **Fire seeks oxygen!** A fire needs heat, fuel, and oxygen to burn. This is called the triangle of fire. If you open a door into a fire with fresh air behind you, the fire will leap toward the oxygen in the event called a backdraft. Never open a door without feeling for heat, and seek other exits if the door is hot.

How Wildfires Start

A wildfire is any unmonitored fire in the wilderness that spreads out of control. It might be a forest fire, a brush fire, or a grass fire. There are three classes of wildland fires. The most common class is the surface fire, which burns along the forest floor, killing or damaging young trees. A ground fire is started by lightning, and burns on or below the forest floor in the humus layer of soil down to the mineral layer. A crown fire jumps along the tops of trees and is spread rapidly by wind.

Aggressive firefighting over the past 100 years has resulted in a buildup of brush and deadwood in many of our forests, providing fuel for fast-spreading, all-consuming wildfires. In addition, many more people now live in the wildland-urban interface—developments where housing

Wildfires can start as brush or leaf fires that are unmonitored and quickly spread. If your community is allowed to burn fall leaves, pictured here, make certain that someone is tending to the burning and has plenty of water handy to pour on the embers when the fire is out.

mixes with natural vegetation. These places are both vulnerable to wildfire and sources of ignition.

The majority of wildfires are caused by humans, deliberately or accidentally, as the following breakdown shows:

- Twenty-six percent are intentionally set to produce habitat for wildlife, enhance hunting, create grazing lands, or kill pests such as chiggers and ticks.

- Nineteen percent are caused by cigarettes, often tossed out of moving cars.

- Eighteen percent are caused by burning debris. Small, controlled fires to burn leaves, deadwood, or trash can spread to the surrounding wilderness if they're left unattended or the wind shifts unexpectedly.

- Nine percent are caused by lightning. There are more than 40,000 lightning storms around the world every day, and about 100 strikes of lightning every second.

- Eight percent are caused by machine use—hot exhaust pipes coming in contact with dry grass, for example.

- Six percent are caused by campfires improperly located, incompletely extinguished, or left burning unattended.

- Fourteen percent are caused by other random events.

Wildfires are literally as fast as the wind. When one breaks out, you have to be prepared to move just as fast.

2 --- Home Fire Prevention and Preparedness

The best way to prepare for a home fire is to try to make sure one never breaks out. Sure, plan an escape route, practice it regularly, and prepare an emergency supply kit—topics covered in chapter 4—but with luck and care, you may never have to put those plans into action.

Safe Cooking Practices

As noted earlier, cooking fires are the number-one cause of home fires. Here are some ways to prevent them:

- Always stay near the stove when cooking. Many fires break out when food is left cooking unattended.

- Avoid wearing loose sleeves while cooking. They can catch on fire from contact with a burner or hot grease.

- Keep all flammable materials away from the stove and oven.

- Never put water on a grease fire. Grease and water don't mix, so water can actually cause the grease to splatter, spreading the fire. Instead, smother the fire with a lid or another pan, and turn off the burner. Leave the pan in place until it has completely cooled. If you try to carry the pan outside, you may leave a trail of flaming grease as you go.

This teenager is using safe cooking practices by standing near the stove while her food is cooking. She is also wearing an insulated mitt, so she will not burn her hand when she touches the pot's hot handle.

Woodstoves and Fireplaces

Woodstoves are cozy and fireplaces are delightful, as long as the fire stays inside them where it belongs. Sadly, that doesn't always happen. Improper use of woodstoves alone causes about 10,800 residential fires every year in the United States. Here are some ways to make certain that you're not part of the statistics:

- Look for solid construction in a woodstove, such as plate steel or cast iron. Inspect it carefully, looking for cracks and making sure all seams are tight.

- Make sure the opening in your fireplace is enclosed with glass doors or a screen with a mesh fine enough to stop sparks and heavy enough to prevent a burning log from rolling out of the fireplace.

- Don't use gasoline, kerosene, or lighter fluid to start a fire.

- Light fires with long-stemmed matches.

- Have your fireplace and chimney, and/or woodstove pipes, inspected annually and cleaned as required.

- Burn only seasoned wood. Burning green wood, some artificial logs, and trash can result in a buildup of creosote in pipes and chimneys. This can catch fire, and increases the risk of carbon monoxide poisoning.

- Make sure the top of your chimney has a guard on it that keeps birds and small animals out, and keeps sparks in.

- Keep newspapers, magazines, rugs, and other flammable objects away from the fireplace.

- Teach children to stay back from the fireplace.

A chimney sweep uses a long-handled brush to clean the creosote from the walls of a chimney. A buildup of the tar-like substance can be highly flammable.

- Never leave a fire unattended.

- Keep a fire extinguisher close at hand.

- Be careful disposing of ashes. Embers can smolder for up to two weeks.

- After a major earthquake, check for cracks in your chimney, where hot embers could get into attic areas.

Portable Heaters

In a cold snap or during winter power outages, many people turn to portable heaters to add to their home's heating. Here are some tips for using portable heaters safely:

- Keep anything that can burn at least three feet (one meter) away from portable heaters.

- Plug electric heaters directly in to outlets, not extension cords.

- Shut off the heater whenever you leave the room or go to bed.

- Make sure your heater has been tested by a reputable organization such as the Underwriters Laboratories Inc. (UL). Check for this on the label or the warranty.

- Never use heaters to dry clothing or anything else.

Electrical Wiring

Faulty wiring, overloaded wall outlets, and damaged extension cords can all cause fires. Keep these tips in mind:

- Be alert for signs of electrical problems. Lights that flicker, fuses that frequently blow, and sparks that shoot from outlets when you plug in or unplug something are all danger signals that require attention from a qualified electrician.

- Never "hot wire" a fuse that has burned out by placing a coin in the socket as a "quick fix."

- Don't run electrical cords under rugs or heavy furniture. The pressure can crack the insulation and break the wires, resulting in sparks that can start a fire.

- Don't overload outlets.

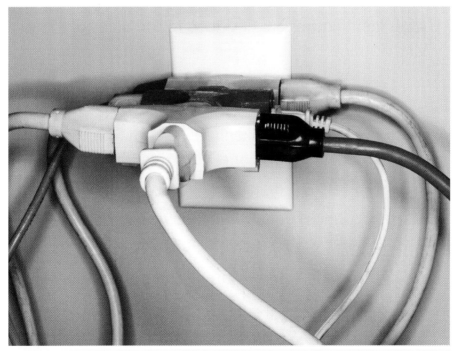

This outlet has too many cords plugged into it and may become overheated. Faulty wiring and overloaded outlets and extension cords can start a fire.

- Always use a ground fault circuit interrupter (GFCI) outlet around water in bathrooms, kitchens, garages, and swimming pools, as well as outdoor receptacles, to prevent electrocution. The GFCI is a superfast circuit breaker that detects ground faults ("leaking" electricity) in a circuit and shuts off power before you can be electrocuted. Moreover, never operate electrical appliances while you are in water; for example, never use a hairdryer while you are taking a bath.

- Don't overload extension cords. If they're warm, they're carrying too much load. Replace them with cords that can handle additional wattage or plug appliances directly in to outlets.

- Most light fixtures are designed to use bulbs of a specific wattage. Do not exceed the maximum wattage.

Appliance Safety

Appliances that are mistakenly believed to be safe cause many fires. Recognize potential hazards and abide by these instructions:

- Many appliances put out heat. Leave plenty of space around them so they can cool properly.

- Make sure your water heater has proper combustion chamber covers.

- In earthquake-prone areas, bolt the water heater top and bottom to wall studs with safety straps to prevent it from tipping over, breaking gas lines, and igniting the gas with the already present flame at the bottom of the water heater.

- Don't pile combustibles near the water heater.

- Regularly clean lint from the dryer cabinet and around the drum. Watch for lint that builds up in the vent line.

- Make sure the stove is off and small appliances are unplugged before you go to bed.

Fire Safety for Smokers

Of course, in terms of health, smoking is never safe for the smoker or those around him or her. But smoking also adds to the risk of a home fire. Smokers should follow these tips:

- Never smoke in bed or anywhere else a person may fall asleep.

- Use deep ashtrays so a lit cigarette can't fall out onto something flammable.

- Never leave a lit cigarette unattended.

- Put some water in ashtrays before emptying them into the trash.

Children and Fire Safety

Children playing with matches cause 5 percent of all residential fires—and are the leading cause of fires that kill children. Some safety rules to obey include the following:

- Don't leave matches and lighters where children can get them—either in the open or in unlocked drawers.

- Don't leave children unattended around lit candles.

- Teach children how to call for emergency help.

- Plug all electrical outlets with safety plugs so children can't stick objects into the outlets.

- Keep children away from the stove and oven while cooking.

Holiday Safety

The winter holiday season is a time of festive decorations, candles, and household upheaval—all of which increase the risk of fire. Here are some holiday fire-safety tips:

This Christmas tree decorated with ornaments adds warm holiday cheer to the room, but the tree is placed near a burning fireplace and could easily ignite.

- If you have a live Christmas tree, make sure it's fresh. Tap the bottom of the trunk against the ground a few times. If the tree is fresh, very few needles will drop off.

- Make certain the tree stand is big enough to support the tree, so there's no danger of the tree falling over. Make sure the reservoir is large, and keep it filled with water so the tree won't dry out. Cut two inches (five centimeters) off the bottom of the tree before putting it in water, so the tree will absorb the water more readily.

- Never place the tree near a heat source.

- Don't block doors or windows (which you might need as escape routes) with a tree or any other decorations.

- Check decorative lights for frayed, broken, or exposed wires.

- Turn off all decorative lights before leaving the house or going to bed.

- Never burn gift-wrapping paper, boxes, or cartons in a fireplace—they burn too quickly and too hot.

- Don't hang stockings on the fireplace mantel when the fireplace is lit.

- Don't use a Christmas tree for firewood.

- Never leave candles unattended. Never place them near combustible materials, such as decorations. And (even though people did it 100 years ago) never use candles to decorate a tree.

Fire-Safety Technology

Even in homes where good fire prevention practices are followed, fires sometimes break out. There are devices that can help limit the damage or at least help you and your family get out safely: fire extinguishers, smoke alarms, carbon monoxide alarms, and home sprinkler systems.

Fire Extinguishers

Every home should have a fire extinguisher (or more than one, depending on the size and layout of the house). Make sure you know where your fire extinguishers are kept—and be sure to read the instructions on them *before* a fire breaks out. Once the flames appear, you may not have time to read!

There are different extinguishers for each of the four classes of fire:

Class A: Fires involving ordinary combustible materials, such as wood, cloth, paper, and many plastics.

Class B: Fires involving flammable liquids and gases, such as gasoline, oil, grease, paint thinner, and propane.

Class C: Fires involving electrical equipment, such as fuse boxes, machinery, appliances, and computers.

Class D: Fires (unlikely to occur in the home) involving burning metals like magnesium or aluminum.

Here are some of the available fire extinguishers:

- Pressurized water extinguishers. These can only be used on class A fires. Using water on other kinds of fires

Fire extinguishers should be a part of every home. There are different extinguishers for each of the four classes of fires. You and your family members should be trained in using an extinguisher. A good time to practice using an extinguisher is just before it expires and is scheduled to be refilled.

can actually intensify the fire, and if the fire involves an electrical appliance, may result in an electric shock. Typically, the water in the canister will spray a stream 15 to 30 feet (4.6 to 9.1 meters) for 30 to 60 seconds.

• Dry chemical extinguishers. Most home fire extinguishers use a dry chemical, but they must be used with care because they produce a dense cloud of dust that can obscure your vision and even cause choking. Some dry chemical extinguishers can be used on class A, B, and C fires. Check the extinguisher's label. Dry chemical extinguishers come in a variety of sizes.

- Carbon dioxide fire extinguishers are used on class B and class C fires, but never on class D fires (because the carbon dioxide can react dangerously with some burning metals). They spray 3 to 8 feet (0.9 to 2.4 m), and suffocate the fire by depriving it of oxygen. However, the gas disperses quickly, so it's important to completely empty the extinguisher and then watch the area to ensure that the fire doesn't reignite.

- Metal/sand extinguishers are used for class D fires. They use powdered copper metal or sodium chloride that will smother the burning metal when sprayed.

Even if you have a fire extinguisher, you shouldn't necessarily use it. Only fight a fire if:

- The fire department has been called.

- Everyone has left the building or is on the way out.

- The fire is small, contained, and doesn't seem to be spreading.

- You have a safe escape route behind you.

- You have the right type of extinguisher for the type of fire you face, and it's working properly.

- You've been trained in using an extinguisher and are confident you know how to use it properly.

All your fire extinguishers should be visually inspected every month, and inspected by a fire-safety company every year.

Smoke Alarms

Too many news stories about fatal fires include the sentence, "There were no working smoke alarms in the house." A simple, inexpensive smoke alarm is the best early fire-detection device available to the average homeowner.

Here are some smoke-alarm tips:

A smoke detector should be located near bedrooms. Many fire departments suggest changing batteries in a smoke detector when daylight savings time occurs, twice each year.

- There should be at least one smoke alarm on every floor of the house.

- Smoke alarms should be placed near bedrooms, on the ceiling, 6 to 12 inches (15.2 to 30.5 centimeters) away from the wall; or on the wall, 6 to 12 inches (15.2 to 30.5 cm) below the ceiling.

- Battery-operated smoke alarms and smoke alarms directly powered by house electrical current both do a good job. You must regularly replace the batteries in a battery-powered smoke alarm. A current-powered smoke alarm often requires an electrician's help to install.

- Keep smoke alarms clean by regularly vacuuming the dust from the alarm vents.

🔥 A Home Fire-Safety Checklist 🔥

Here's a handy home fire-safety checklist you can use to see how vulnerable your house is to fire:

✓ Is there a smoke alarm on each floor?

✓ Is there a carbon monoxide alarm near the bedrooms?

✓ If the alarms are battery operated, are their batteries checked regularly and replaced annually?

✓ If the alarms are powered by house current, are they checked periodically to be sure they work?

✓ Are the fire extinguishers easily accessible and are they fully charged?

✓ Are they inspected annually by a qualified technician?

✓ Are any extension cords overloaded?

✓ Are any electrical cords running under rugs or furniture?

✓ Is the house wiring up to code?

✓ Do you have surge protector bars on air conditioners, entertainment equipment, and computers?

✓ Is the furnace checked and cleaned annually?

✓ Are the filters changed regularly?

✓ Are the fireplace and chimney cleaned and checked annually?

✓ Is the fireplace damper functioning?

✓ Does the fireplace have proper doors or a screen?

✓ Is all flammable material properly stored away from sources of heat?

✓ Is the water heater bolted to the wall in earthquake-prone areas?

✓ Is there a gas wrench attached to the gas meter for fast turn-off after earthquakes?

✓ Have children been taught how to call 911 and report a fire by giving their name, address, and situation?

✓ Does everyone know how to stay low to the floor where air is safer when escaping a fire?

✓ Are matches and lighters stored out of the reach of children?

- Press each smoke alarm's test button monthly to make sure the alarm is still in good working condition.

Carbon Monoxide Alarms

Malfunctioning appliances and heaters, and clogged stovepipes and chimneys pose another hazard besides fire risk: they can flood the home with carbon monoxide. For that reason, every home should also have at least one carbon monoxide alarm near the sleeping area, and ideally, at least one on each level of the home.

Never use charcoal briquettes inside a house, tent, or trailer because the burning briquettes use up the room's oxygen and give off poisonous carbon monoxide. Carbon monoxide is a colorless, odorless gas. Low-level exposure to it can cause headaches, nausea, dizziness, and fatigue. Higher levels of exposure can be fatal. Many fatalities occur when people are asleep, because carbon monoxide puts people into a deeper sleep from which they may never wake up.

Home Fire Sprinkler Systems

Most of us have seen fire sprinkler systems in commercial and public buildings. When triggered by heat, they set off a spray of water, dousing flames before they can spread, and limiting the damage from smoke and heat.

Many new houses are being built with home fire sprinkler systems. Older homes can be retrofitted with them, usually during other renovation work. The cost of installing a sprinkler system during new construction is around $1 per square foot (0.09 square meter).

3 --- Wildfire Prevention and Preparedness

A home fire affects a single house. A wildfire can threaten or destroy an entire neighborhood, or even an entire town.

The first step toward being properly prepared for wildfires is to contact your local fire department, health department, and forestry office to find out what the community plans are in the event of a wildfire—and how you can help make sure those plans can be carried out effectively. Report any hazardous conditions you've noticed to the proper authorities. Find out what the local regulations are for burning leaves or other rubbish, and follow them.

One important consideration is access to your land. Make sure that fire equipment can get onto your property—and make sure that your name and address are clearly displayed at all driveway entrances.

Make Neighborhood Plans

You should plan ahead of time about how people in the neighborhood can work together in the event of a wildfire, and afterward. Here are some suggestions:

- Talk to your neighbors about wildfire safety, and how you can all work to make it harder for fires to spread.

- Make a list of any special medical or technical skills of people in the neighborhood, as well as any equipment

This roadside sign in a Lake Tahoe, California, area warns motorists of the chances of a forest fire starting on that day. If a neighborhood does not have a community plan for fire preparedness, neighbors should make a plan for helping one another before a wildfire occurs.

they might have that could be useful when fire threatens—or after it has come and gone.

- Make a neighborhood plan for helping people with special needs, such as elderly people or people with disabilities. Include a signal system, such as signs in the window saying "HELP" or "OK" to let neighbors know their situation.

- Make a neighborhood plan for taking care of children who may be on their own if their parents can't get home.

- Pre-identify neighborhood water sources, such as swimming pools, that could be used to fight fires.

Fire-Safe Landscaping

Everyone in communities that are vulnerable to wildfires should be practicing fire-safe landscaping. The goal of fire-safe landscaping is to reduce the amount of fuel available for a wildfire close to your home. You should create a safety zone that extends 30 to 50 feet (9.1–15.2 m) out from your home in all directions (or a minimum of 100 feet [30.5 m] if you live in a pine forest).

Within the safety zone, carry out these guidelines:

- Clear away flammable vegetation (for example, plants that have a high oil, high resin, or low moisture content, such as junipers, cedars, eucalypti, cypresses, dry grasses, and sagebrushes), and regularly rake up all leaves, dead limbs, and twigs.

- Remove all leaves and rubbish that may have collected under any structures.

- Space trees at least 30 feet (9.1 m) apart and prune all branches to a height of 8 to 10 feet (2.4–3 m).

- Remove any dead tree branches that extend over the roof of the house.

- Cut away any tree branches or shrubs that have grown within 15 feet (4.6 m) of a stovepipe or chimney.

- Have the power company clear away any branches that are near power lines.

- Remove any vines that are growing on structures.

- Keep the grass of the lawn well cut.

- When choosing landscaping for your home, select fire-resistant plants. Local plant nurseries can tell you what fire-resistant species are suited for your environment. In general, hardwood trees (such as maple, poplar, and cherry) are less flammable than conifers (pines and firs).

- Keep plants that are growing nearby green. Water them well during the dry season.

- Clear the area within 10 feet (3 m) of any propane tanks.

- Don't let newspapers or trash pile up—dispose of it.

- Store gasoline, oily rags, and other flammable materials in approved safety cans, and place the cans in a protected location away from the bases of any buildings.

- Stack firewood at least 100 feet (30.5 m) away from your home.

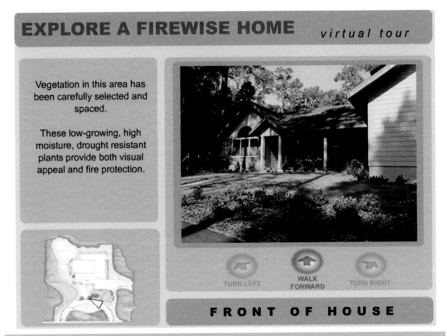

EXPLORE A FIREWISE HOME *virtual tour*

Vegetation in this area has been carefully selected and spaced.

These low-growing, high moisture, drought resistant plants provide both visual appeal and fire protection.

TURN LEFT   WALK FORWARD   TURN RIGHT

F R O N T   O F   H O U S E

This screen shot from the Web page for Firewise (www.firewise.org), an online site that contains educational information for people who live in fire-prone regions of the United States, shows homeowners how to make a fire-safe landscape.

- Keep fire tools close at hand: a rake, an axe, a handsaw or chain saw, a bucket, and a shovel.

- Keep a ladder on hand that will enable you to reach the roof of your house or other structures.

- Make sure a campfire is not left burning by using plenty of water and stirring the coals with a stick. Hot coals can be ignited by the wind, even after twenty-four to forty-eight hours, starting a wildfire!

Don't Forget the Water!

If a fire breaks out, your family and the fire department will need water to fight it. Make sure you have an adequate outside water source—a fire hydrant, pond, cistern, well, or swimming pool. Make sure your garden hose is long enough to reach all parts of your home and any other structures. And if possible, you should have a portable gasoline-powered pump; electrical power is often cut off during wildfires.

If you live in a cold climate, it's important to have freeze-proof exterior water outlets on at least two sides of your home and near any other structures. Additional outlets at least 50 feet (15.2 m) from the house are a good idea, too.

Keeping the House Fire Safe

There are also some things that can be done to protect the house itself. Here are some tips:

- Regularly clean the roof and gutters. Leaves and other debris can catch fire if flying embers land on them.

- Screen off the areas underneath porches, decks, and the home itself; and screen all openings to the floors, roof, and attic. Use a mesh no bigger than 1/8 inch (3.2 millimeters). This will help keep embers from finding their way inside the structure.

- Consider installing metal or fireproof shutters or heavy, fire-resistant drapes. Again, this can help keep out flying embers.

- Consider installing multipaned windows. Not only are these more energy efficient, but if the outer pane breaks, the inner pane provides one more layer of defense against fire.

4 --- Escaping a Fire

Practicing fire safety can reduce the risk of fire, but can't eliminate it completely. Wildfires in particular are out of your control. When fire threatens, the focus becomes safety. You need to know how to get out of your house, or how to evacuate your property efficiently, quickly, and safely. The key is preparation.

Escaping a Home Fire

It's hard to think clearly in a fire, so it's important to have a well-rehearsed plan in place ahead of time.

- Make a diagram of your house. Mark all the windows and doors, and plan two routes out of every room.

- Think about various scenarios. How will you get out if the fire is in the kitchen? In the basement? In a bedroom?

- If you live in a two- or three-story house with bedrooms on the upper floors, buy escape ladders. Learn how to use them, and store them near windows that can be used as emergency exits. If you have security bars on your windows, make sure they have quick-release devices so they can be opened immediately in an emergency.

- Once you have your escape scenarios figured out, practice them from every room in the house, several times to begin with, then at least twice each year. Actually set off the smoke alarm so you will recognize the sound even at night if you are awakened.

- Specify a location outside where everyone will meet: for example, under a specific tree, or at the end of the driveway. That ensures that the family knows where everyone is, and no one gets hurt looking for someone who has already escaped.

If a fire breaks out, follow these steps:

- Get out first, then call the fire department from a cell phone or a phone at a neighbor's house. Make sure everyone in the family knows how to call for emergency assistance, but designate one person to do so.

- Once you're out, stay out! Never go back into a burning building.

- If smoke or fire blocks your first escape route from a room, use the second.

- If you have to exit through smoke, crawl. Smoke rises, so the air is clearer near the floor.

- Make sure everyone knows how to "stop, drop, and roll." If clothing catches fire, stop, drop to the floor or ground, and roll over and over or back and forth until the fire is extinguished.

- If you're escaping through a closed door, feel it first. If it's warm, don't open it. Use your second way out. If it

Participants in a fire-safety drill at a college dormitory are crawling along the floor of a smoke-filled hallway. Smoke rises during a fire, so the clearest air to breathe is near the floor.

feels cool, brace your shoulder against it and open it slowly. If heat and smoke come in, slam it securely closed, then use your second escape route.

- If both exit routes are blocked, stay in the room with the door closed. Hang a brightly colored cloth out the window to attract attention. If there's a working phone in the room, use it to tell the fire department that you're trapped and where you are.

Help for People with Special Needs

Escaping from a home fire can be complicated by the special needs of small children, elderly persons, and disabled people. Here are some tips for helping people with special needs:

- If there are babies or toddlers in the home, figure out the best way to get them out. Train older siblings to help evacuate younger brothers and sisters. Keeping a baby harness near the crib allows someone to carry a baby while keeping his or her hands free to help older children.

- Have an escape plan that takes into consideration the possibility that one parent or guardian might be away.

- Teach children how to cover their nose and mouth to reduce the amount of smoke they inhale.

- Once they're old enough, teach them to crawl under the smoke and what the escape routes are.

- Make sure all exits are clear of toys.

- People with decreased mobility should ideally have their bedrooms on the ground floor, and as close as possible to an exit.

- If someone in the house is confined to a wheelchair, consider adding a ramp to the entrances of the home. Be sure that wheelchairs and walkers fit through all possible exits; if they don't, the doorways should be widened to accommodate them. Create a buddy system to help people with special needs evacuate the building.

- In your escape plans, decide who is responsible for helping those with special needs and practice the steps necessary for getting them safely out of the house.

Remember that people who are hearing impaired may not be able to hear a smoke or fire alarm. Special smoke alarms can indicate the presence of smoke by flashing lights or a vibrating pad.

Safety of Pets

It's a hard lesson, but an important one: the safety of a pet is never as important as the safety of a person. If a pet can be safely picked up or released outside during an evacuation, great. (It is even better if the pet can be quickly leashed or otherwise restrained first.) However, many pets will go into hiding in the event of a fire. If you don't see the pet immediately, get outside, then tell the firefighters that there is a pet inside and where it is likely to be found. (It's a good idea to make a list of your pet's favorite sleeping and hiding places.)

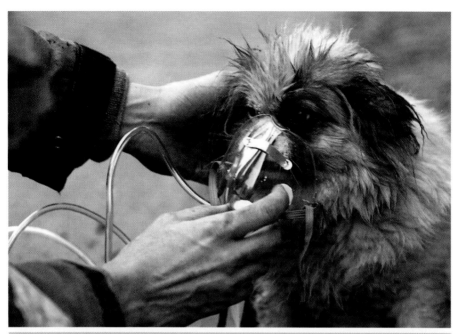

A firefighter gives a dog a dose of oxygen after the dog was rescued from a house fire in North Carolina. Remember that the safety of a pet is never as important as the safety of a person. If your pet is rescued safely, make sure your veterinarian checks him or her carefully, because pets can have burns under their fur.

Many pet stores offer stickers for your door that also inform firefighters or emergency workers there may be a pet inside.

After a fire, have your pet checked by a veterinarian as soon as possible. Pets can suffer smoke inhalation just like humans, and can sometimes suffer burns under their fur.

Apartment and High-Rise Fires

Most of this book has focused on fires in single-family homes, but many people live in apartment or condominium complexes, ranging from one story to the size of a skyscraper.

There should be a set escape plan for any multifamily building, with well-marked fire exits, fire marshals who help ensure that everyone gets out of the building, and a planned gathering space for everyone once they are outside. Regular fire drills should be held.

In a high-rise, these are some special safety steps to take:

- Learn the sound of your building's fire alarm.

- Know who is responsible for maintaining the fire-safety systems. Keep an eye out for potential problems and report them promptly.

- Never lock fire exits or doorways in halls or stair-ways. Never prop fire doors open. Fire doors slow the spread of fire and smoke.

- If you discover a fire, pull your building's fire alarm, then get out.

- If the fire alarm sounds, don't assume anyone else has called the fire department. The fire department would rather have everyone in the building call than no one call. Give the dispatcher any information that is requested.

- Before leaving your apartment, feel the door with the back of your hand. If it feels warm, don't open it; check your second escape route, and if that is not an option, then stay put. Stuff cracks around the door with towels, rags, or tape to keep out smoke. Cover any vents. If you have a phone, call the fire department and tell them exactly where you are and that you are trapped. Then wait at a window and signal with a light or by waving a sheet. Open the window at top and bottom if you can, but don't break it—you may need to close it if smoke rushes in. Don't panic, and be patient. Rescuing every-one in a high-rise building can take several hours.

• If the door is not warm, open it slightly while staying low to the floor. If there is no smoke, you can leave your apartment and follow the evacuation plan.

• Never use an elevator in a fire; always use the stairs.

Escaping a Wildfire

Wildfires are different from home fires in that you usually have some warning that one is threatening your area. However, that warning may be limited to just a few hours, and the order to evacuate may leave you with only minutes to get out, so it's important to be ready.

Keep your emergency supply kit (see page 44) where it can be gathered quickly if you have to evacuate.

What to Do When Wildfire Threatens

When a wildfire threatens, complete the following steps:

• Listen to the radio for news reports and evacuation instructions. Follow those instructions! If told to evacu-ate, do so immediately.

• Make sure the car is backed into the garage or is parked facing the direction of escape. Make sure the doors are closed and unlocked and the windows are rolled up (to keep out flying embers). Leave the key in the ignition.

YOUR EMERGENCY SUPPLY KIT

These supplies are useful not only in the case of a wildfire, but in cases of other natural disasters that may force an evacuation. Pack the supplies into sturdy, easy-to-carry containers such as backpacks. Your kit should include:

✓ A three-day supply of water, one gallon per person per day.

✓ Food and beverages that won't spoil, such as canned meats, fruits, and vegetables. (Don't forget a nonelectric can opener!)

✓ Food and water for pets.

✓ One change of clothing and footwear per person.

✓ One blanket or sleeping bag per person.

✓ A first-aid kit. This kit should include essential items such as bandages of various sizes, sterilized gauze pads, antiseptic wipes, adhesive tape, antibacterial salve, scissors, tweezers, and a face shield that can be used as a CPR breathing barrier.

✓ An emergency supply of prescription medications, copies of the doctor's prescriptions, and a copy of your medical coverage card to get refills.

✓ A battery-operated radio.

✓ A flashlight and extra batteries.

✓ An extra set of car keys.

✓ A credit card, cash, or travelers' checks.

✓ Toilet paper, soap, and other hygienic supplies.

✓ Items such as disposable diapers, baby food, formula for infants, and items for people with special needs, such as hearing aids and extra eyeglasses.

✓ Copies of important documents in a fire-proof waterproof container.

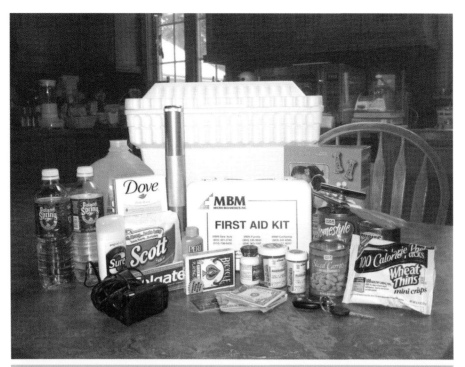

A disaster supply kit should be prepared in every household. Make sure your kit includes a three-day supply of water. Your kit should be kept in a sturdy container and in a place where it is easy to grab during an emergency. Ensure that everyone in the house is familiar with the kit's location.

- If the car is in the garage, close the garage windows and doors to protect the structure, but leave them unlocked.

- If you have pets, confine them to a room where you can find them readily (and if you have cats and dogs, do not confine them to the same room).

- Arrange temporary housing somewhere outside the area threatened by fire.

- Remember to evacuate downhill, because fire climbs uphill, as heat rises.

- Dress in protective clothing: sturdy shoes and clothing such as long pants and a long-sleeved shirt. Gloves can protect your hands, and a handkerchief can protect your face.

- Close windows, vents, and doors. If you have fire-safe shutters or fire-resistant blinds, close them. Remove any lightweight, flammable curtains.

- Shut off the gas to your house at the meter and turn off all pilot lights.

- Open the fireplace damper and close the fireplace screens.

- Move flammable furniture to the center of the home, away from windows and glass doors.

- Turn on all the lights to make your house more visible in thick smoke.

- Seal any exterior vents. You can precut plywood for this purpose, or purchase commercially made seals ahead of time.

- Turn off propane tanks.

- Move combustible outdoor furniture inside.

- Connect your garden hose to the outside tap.

- Set up the portable gasoline-powered pump (if you have one) to pump water in case the power goes off.

- Wet the roof with a hose or by placing lawn sprinklers on it.

To help protect his home during the Piru fire in October 2003, a homeowner in Fillmore, California, wets his roof. Firefighters thought they had contained the surrounding fire, but the fire flared up again. If possible, in the event of a fire, people should use a lawn sprinkler on the roof to help wet it.

In 2002, in Show Low, Arizona, as a wildfire burns out of control, residents evacuate the town after local authorities issued a mandatory order to leave. If authorities order an evacuation, leave immediately, but make sure you choose a route that takes you away from the fire. Fire officials will have routes planned for an emergency evacuation.

- Wet or remove any shrubs within 15 feet (4.6 m) of the house.

If the order comes to evacuate, it might come with very short notice. If so, leave immediately, taking your emergency supply kit and locking your home behind you. Make sure somebody outside the threatened area, or the authorities, knows that you have left, where you are going, and what route you're taking. And make sure you choose a route away from the fire. Keep alert for changes in the speed and direction of the fire and smoke.

Get away from the affected area, and stay away until the local authorities tell you it's safe to return. Only then should you go back to see what damage, if any, the wildfire has caused to your home. In addition, try to be understanding of the firefighters and local officials' decisions—their main goal is to get the wildfires under control, and they may not be able to save every home.

5 --- After a Fire

Whether a fire starts inside your home or spreads to it during a wildfire, you'll find yourself returning to a damaged home. What you'll need or be able to do after that depends on the extent of the damage.

The First Twenty-four Hours

For immediate needs, such as temporary housing, food, or clothing, you should contact your local disaster relief service, typically the American Red Cross.

You should also contact your insurance agent or company and follow their advice. (And be sure to save receipts for any money you spend after you've been forced out of your home; you'll need them for your insurance company and taxes.)

Let the police know that your home is unoccupied, especially if it is damaged and therefore vulnerable to trespassers. You should also inform them of your new location (at a friend's house, motel, or shelter). Also tell your insurance company, mortgage company (which also needs to know about the fire), extended family and friends, employers, schools, the post office, any delivery services, the fire department, and your utility companies where your family can now be found.

Don't try to enter the house. Fires can rekindle unexpectedly from hidden hot spots. The fire department will

🔥 Did They Have to Do That? 🔥

Sometimes people return home to what appears to be a relatively undamaged house—except for the holes knocked in the walls and roof by the firefighters themselves!

Did they have to do that?

Well, yes, they did.

Fires move up first, then outward, as they burn. By breaking windows or cutting holes in the roof, firefighters are able to keep the fire burning upward, rather than spreading outward. This "ventilation" also helps clear the building of smoke, allowing the firefighters to fight the fire more effectively.

Making holes in the walls is also necessary to ensure that the fire is completely out and that it isn't still burning out of sight inside the walls or other hidden places. The holes help prevent potentially worse damage to the structure in the long run.

A volunteer firefighter chops through the roof of a burning attic during a house fire in Texas. Making a hole in the roof will help vent the fire, to keep it burning upward, rather than spreading outward. Such holes also help clear the smoke out of the building.

normally disconnect any utilities (electricity, water, and gas), or make sure they're safe to use before they leave the site. If a utility is turned off, don't try to turn it on yourself.

Watch for structural damage. Roofs and floors may be in danger of collapse.

Don't try to salvage food, beverages, or medicines that have been exposed to heat, smoke, soot, or water because they may not be safe for consumption.

Don't throw away anything until a complete inventory of the property has been taken: the insurance company will take all

These family members in New Mexico had to evacuate their home during a wildfire. After a fire, never try to reenter your home without being given the OK by authorities and inspecting the extent of the damage first.

damages into consideration when developing your family's claim. Discuss any salvage or repair plans that your family members have with the insurance company first. (There are companies that specialize in the restoration of fire-damaged structures.)

If your family rents, contact the landlord, because it is the owner's responsibility to prevent further loss or damage to the site. Secure your personal belongings or move them to another location if possible.

If your family's property is not insured, you may have to rely on your own resources or community agencies for assistance. Some organizations that can be of help

🔥 Document Recovery 🔥

Among the many things you and your family may have to replace after a fire are valuable documents and records. Here's a checklist that may be useful:

Item	Whom to contact
Driver's license and auto registration	Department of Motor Vehicles
Bank records	Your bank
Insurance policies	Your insurance agent
Military discharge papers	Department of Veterans Affairs
Passports	Passport service office, the U.S. Department of State
Birth, marriage, and death certificates	Bureau of Records in the appropriate state
Divorce papers	Circuit court where decree was issued
Social Security or Medicare cards	Local Social Security office
Credit cards	Whatever companies issued the cards, as soon as possible
Titles to deeds	Records department of the locality in which the property is located
Stocks and bonds	Issuing company or your broker
Wills	Your lawyer
Medical records	Your doctor or hospital
Warranties	Companies that issued them
Income tax records	The Internal Revenue Service center where you file, or your accountant
Citizenship papers	U.S. Immigration and Naturalization Service
Prepaid burial contract	Company that issued it
Animal registration papers	Humane Society or your veterinarian
Mortgage papers	Lending institution

include the American Red Cross, the Salvation Army, local churches, the department of social services, various civic organizations, and state or municipal emergency services offices.

Replacing Currency

Your family may have paper and coin currency severely damaged in a fire. Handle any burned money as little as possible. Place each bill or portion of a bill in plastic wrap. If half or more of a bill is intact, you can take it to your regional Federal Reserve Bank for a replacement (ask your own bank for the location of the nearest regional Federal

An insurance agent works on a claim after a house fire. Always have your family contact the insurance company immediately after you and your home have been involved in a fire. Be sure to take photographs of the damage and save all receipts for any expenses you have after you've evacuated your home.

Reserve Bank). Your regional Federal Reserve Bank will also accept mutilated or melted coins.

Savings bonds that have been destroyed or mutilated must be replaced by the U.S. Department of the Treasury. Your local bank will have the necessary form, or you can find it at http://www.ustreas.gov, along with mailing instructions.

Be Prepared

Anyone can become a victim of fire, no matter where they are or where they live. You can lessen the risk with some of the fire-safety tips in this book, but you can't remove it entirely. If fire does strike, though, you can increase the likelihood that you and your family will survive it, and ensure that you recover from it more quickly, by adopting the motto "Be prepared." You don't have to be a member of the Boy Scouts of America to know that this is good advice.

Glossary

backdraft A confined fire that jumps quickly through an opening toward oxygen.

carbon dioxide A colorless, odorless gas that is sometimes used to put out fires. Although it can't be breathed, it is nonpoisonous (unlike carbon monoxide).

carbon monoxide A colorless, odorless gas that can cause headaches, nausea, dizziness, and fatigue. High levels of exposure can be fatal.

combustibles Objects or substances that readily catch fire.

creosote A dark brown or black flammable tar that builds up on the walls of a chimney, primarily from wood smoke.

ember A glowing fragment of hot fuel from a fire, capable of igniting other flammable materials.

evacuate To leave one place for another for safety reasons.

fire-safe landscaping Reducing the amount of fuel available for a wildfire close to a building, primarily by clearing away flammable vegetation.

flammable Capable of catching fire easily and burning rapidly.

flashover point The temperature at which everything flammable in a room bursts into flames at once.

fuel Anything that can burn. Fires need fuel, heat, and oxygen to keep burning.

GFCI (ground fault circuit interrupter) A superfast circuit breaker that detects ground faults in a circuit and shuts off electricity before a person can be electrocuted.

humus A brown or black mixture in topsoil that is the result of the partial decomposition of plant or animal matter and that provides nutrients for living plants.

oxygen The colorless, odorless, tasteless gas that is present in the air we breathe, and that fires need to burn.

receptacle An electrical outlet for a plug.

smoke alarm A device that makes a loud noise (or sometimes flashes a light or vibrates a pad) in the presence of even a small amount of smoke.

space heater A portable heater used to warm an enclosed space, such as a single room.

wildfire Any unmonitored fire in a wilderness area that spreads out of control.

For More Information

American Red Cross National Headquarters
2025 E Street NW
Washington, DC 20006
(202) 303-4498
Web site: http://www.redcross.org

Canadian Centre for Emergency Preparedness
77 James Street North, Suite 325
Hamilton, ON L8R 2K3
Canada
Web site: http://www.ccep.ca

Federal Emergency Management Agency (FEMA)
500 C Street SW
Washington, DC 20472
(800) 621-FEMA
Web site: http://www.fema.gov

The Firefighters Burn Fund, Inc. (Staying Alive)
207 Eastmount Drive
Winnipeg, MB
Canada
R2N 3W9
(204) 256-9351
Web site: http://www.stayingalive.ca

Firewise Headquarters
1 Batterymarch Park
Quincy, MA 02269
(617) 984-7486
Web site: http://www.firewise.org

National Fire Protection Association
1 Batterymarch Park
Quincy, MA 02269
(617) 770-3000
Web site: http://www.nfpa.org

United States Fire Administration
Office of Fire Management Programs
16825 South Seton Avenue
Emmitsburg, MD 21727
(301) 447-1000
Web site: http://www.usfa.fema.gov

Web Sites

Due to the changing nature of Internet links, the Rosen Publishing Group, Inc., has developed an online list of Web sites related to the subject of this book. This site is updated regularly. Please use this link to access the list:

www.rosenlinks.com/lep/fiwi

For Further Reading

Beil, Karen Magnuson. *Fire in Their Eyes: Wildfires and the People Who Fight Them*. San Diego, CA: Harcourt, 1999.

Bryan, Nichol. *Los Alamos: Wildfires* (Environmental Disasters). Milwaukee, WI: Gareth Stevens, 2003.

Cottrell, William H. *The Book of Fire*. Missoula, MT: Mountain Press, 2005.

Diamantes, David. *Principles of Fire Prevention*. Clifton Park, NY: Thomson Delmar Learning, 2005.

Gorrell, Gena. *Catching Fire: The Story of Firefighting*. Toronto, ON: Tundra Books, 1999.

Maclean, John N. *Fire and Ashes: On the Front Lines of American Wildfires*. New York, NY: Henry Holt, 2003.

Maze, Stephanie, and Catherine O'Neill Grace. *I Want to Be . . . a Firefighter*. San Diego, CA: Harcourt, 1999.

Rodriguez, Ana Maria, ed. *Fires* (Great Disasters). San Diego, CA: Greenhaven Press, 2004.

Simon, Seymour. *Wildfires*. New York, NY: HarperTrophy, 2000.

White, Katherine. *The 2000–2002 Forest Fires in the Western United States* (Tragic Fires Throughout History). New York, NY: Rosen Publishing, 2004.

Bibliography

"Are You Ready: Fires." Fema.com. Retrieved June 1, 2005 (http://www.fema.gov/areyouready/fire.shtm).

Bates, Karen Grigsby. "Interview: Vicki Clapp describes her experience having to evacuate her home from an approaching wildfire." NPR Special. October 28, 2003. Retrieved August 9, 2005 (http://www.npr.org/templates/story/story.php?storyId=1481859).

Cottrell, William H. *The Book of Fire.* Missoula, MT: Mountain Press, 2005.

"Disaster Preparation." MetLife Life Advice. Retrieved June 1, 2005 (http://www.metlife.com/Applications/Corporate/WPS/CDA/PageGenerator/0,1674,P801,00.html).

"Disaster Services." American Red Cross. Retrieved June 1, 2005 (http://www.redcross.org/services/disaster/0,1082,_319_,00.html).

Diamantes, David. *Principles of Fire Prevention.* Clifton Park, NY: Thomson Delmar Learning, 2005.

"Explore a Firewise Home: Virtual Tour." Retrieved June 1, 2005 (http://www.firewise.org/vrhome/).

Field, Frank, and John Morse. *Dr. Frank Field's Get Out Alive: Save Your Family's Life with Fire Survival Techniques.* New York, NY: Random House, 1992.

Fuller, Margaret. *Forest Fires: An Introduction to Wildland Fire Behavior: Management, Firefighting, and Prevention.* New York, NY: John Wiley and Sons, 1991.

"Home Escape Plan." *Staying Alive.* In Cooperation with the Firefighters' Burn Fund Inc. Retrieved June 1, 2005 (http//www.stayingalive.ca/home_escape_plan.html).

Jaffe, Matthew, "Living with Wildfire." *Sunset Magazine.* April 1, 2001. Retrieved June 1, 2005 (http://www.sunset.com/sunset/Premium/ Home/2001/04-Apr/Fire0401/FireIntro2003.html).

Larson, Travis, "Seven unexpected ways fires start: most heartbreaking losses are surprisingly easy to prevent," *The Family Handyman.* May 1, 2002, pp. 74–84.

"Personal Preparedness." Canadian Centre for Emergency Preparedness. Retrieved June 1, 2005 (http://www.ccep.ca/cceppers.html).

"Wildfires." Bell Museum of Natural History. Retrieved June 1, 2005 (http://www.bellmuseum.org/wildfire.html).

Index

A

animals/pets, 5–6, 40–41, 44, 45, 52

apartment and high-rise fires, 41–43

appliance safety, 20–21

B

backdraft, 12

C

campfires, 14, 34

carbon monoxide alarms, 24, 28, 29

children
and fire safety, 21–22, 28
help for during a fire, 32, 39

cigarettes/smoking, 8, 14, 21

conditions in a fire, 9–12

cooking practices, 15

D

document recovery, 52

E

earthquake, 18, 20, 28

elderly/disabled persons, 39, 40

electrical wiring, tips on, 18–20

emergency kit, 15, 43, 44, 48

F

fire extinguishers, 28
types of, 24–26

firefighting
and damaging homes, 50
when to attempt, 26
in wilderness, 13

fireplaces, 4, 16–18, 23, 28, 46

fire-safety checklist, 28

fire-safety quiz, 11–12

fireworks, 9

first-aid kit, 44

flashover point, 10

G

gas poisoning, 12, 17, 29
symptoms of, 29

grease fires, 7, 11, 12, 15, 24

H

holidays, 8–9, 22–23

home fires, causes of, 7–9

house maintenance, 35

I

insurance, 49, 51, 52

L

landscaping, 32–34
lightning, 13, 14

M

money, burned, 53–54

N

National Fire Protection
    Association (NFPA), 7, 12
neighborhood plans, 30

P

portable heaters, 7–8, 18

S

smoke alarms, 12, 24, 27–29, 37
    for the hearing impaired, 40
sprinkler systems, 24, 29
statistics, 6, 7, 14, 16, 21

W

water heaters, 20–21, 28
wildfires
    California 2003, 4–6
    causes of, 13–14
    classes of, 13
    definition of, 12–13
    what to do, 43–48
woodstoves, 16–18

About the Author

Edward Willett writes a weekly science column for the *Regina Leader Post* and CBC Radio, and is the author of more than thirty books on a variety of subjects. He has had a lifelong interest in fire and fire prevention. As a child, he witnessed two large fires, one near his kindergarten and one in a factory near his home. As a newspaper reporter, he photographed and reported on fires and their aftermath many times, and as a newspaper editor, he oversaw special fire prevention sections annually for several years. He lives in Regina, Saskatchewan, Canada.

Photo Credits

Cover, p. 1 © Mark Avery/Orange County Register/Corbis; pp. 5, 9, 17, 38, 41, 47, 50, 53 © AP/ Wide World Photos; p. 10 © Peter Hvizdak/The Image Works; p. 13 © Philip Gould/ Corbis; p. 16 © Esbin-Anderson/The Image Works; p. 19 © John Wilkes Studio/Corbis; p. 22 © Dennis Degnan/Corbis; p. 25 Louis Moses/Corbis; p. 27 © The Image Works Archive; p. 31 © Marty Heitner/The Image Works; p. 34 http://www. firewise.org/vrhome/; p. 45 by Tahara Anderson; pp. 48, 51 © Reuters/Corbis.

Designer: Tahara Anderson
Editor: Kathy Kuhtz Campbell